English text **Alison Winn**

**HODDER AND STOUGHTON**

LONDON SYDNEY AUCKLAND TORONTO

Gunilla Wolde

# Emma and the vacuum cleaner

When Daddy vacuums the carpet, Emma likes to sit on the back of the cleaner. She pretends it is a funny fat animal with a whirring noise in its tummy.

Emma knows how Daddy makes the whirring noise start. All he has to do is to press a little button.
Emma mustn't ever switch the vacuum on herself.

Sometimes, when Daddy is using the vacuum cleaner, he lets Emma help. It's fun to watch the puffy balls of fluff roll into tiny little sausages, just as the cleaner gobbles them up.

Tiny specks of sand, that Emma can hardly see at all, make a scratchy sound as they disappear.

Now – what was that?
With a rattle and a clatter,
a button and a Lego brick
are sucked inside
the cleaner.

A little bit of paper tries to escape.
Emma gives it a little push, and it flutters
down the tube like
all the other things.

But Teddy is much too fat to get gobbled up. The cleaner makes a louder whirring noise when Teddy's tummy gets stuck in the hole. Daddy and Emma both think it is *not* a good idea to vacuum Teddy.

Emma's hair flutters about
near the mouth of the
cleaner. But it's stuck
firmly to her head, which is
a good thing.
Emma knows that *she* is too
big to get gobbled up by
the cleaner.

And what about baby brother?
*You* can see that *he* is too big.
But when Emma pretends to vacuum him up,
he is scared and shouts "Daddy, Daddy, Daddy".

So Emma vacuums his sock instead.
It is sucked into the hole with a loud "glump".

Poor baby brother – he cries when he sees
his sock disappear.
Emma hopes she can get it back.
Where is it? – it must be inside the
vacuum cleaner.

Daddy switches off the electricity and
takes out the plug. He tells Emma how to take
the cover off the cleaner.

Inside the cleaner,
there is a bag, and
inside the bag is a
lot of dust and
rubbish – but no sock.

Emma shakes the bag hard. Look,
out tumbles the sand –
the fluff – the Lego brick – the
button – *and* baby brother's sock!

Baby brother *is* glad to have
his sock back again.

But Emma looks at Daddy. She wonders if he is glad to see all the dust and rubbish on the carpet.

However did the sock get so quickly down the long tube and inside the bag?
To find out, we'll pretend the vacuum cleaner is made of glass. See! the yellow arrows pretend to be baby brother's sock, and the blue arrows are air.
When the button is pressed, two fans whizz round inside the cleaner, and suck in air through the long tube.

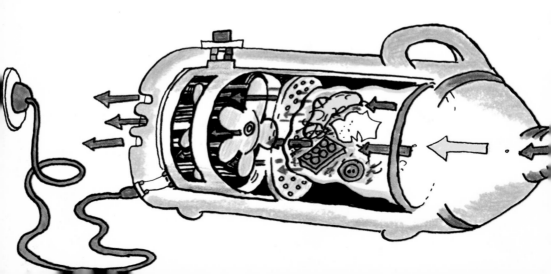

The little fans make such a strong draught,
that it sucks all the bits and pieces
down the long tube into the cleaner's tummy.
When the air goes out again, it leaves behind
the sand, the fluff, the paper, the button,
the Lego brick *and* baby brother's sock.

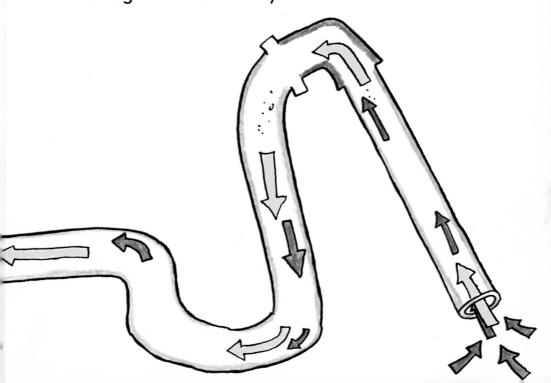

Daddy tells Emma how to fix the cover back on the cleaner. Now she knows that *some* things must not be sucked away. Next time she uses the vacuum, she will be more careful, I hope.

Daddy switches on the electricity and Emma
cleans up all the rubbish she tipped out of
the bag, when she was
looking for baby
brother's sock.

Funny! Now baby brother *likes* the vacuum cleaner. But only when Daddy has switched it off and the noise has stopped. He pretends he is riding on a funny fat animal. He makes his own whirring noise with his mouth.